MAGIC TALES

Blue Dragoon Books

Magic Tales

Blue Dragoon Books

Cover designed & Illustrations by Blye Dragoon Books

Edited by Blue Dragoon Books

Published by Blue Dragoon Books

Copyright The Little French's Media

Published 2023

Once upon a time, in a land far, far away, there was a magical kingdom ruled by a wise and powerful king, who had magic in his veins. He could control the elements, speak to animals, and make the stars dance in the sky.

Everyone in the kingdom was in awe of the King's magical abilities and respected him greatly. However, some were envious of his powers and coveted them for themselves.

One day, a sorcerer named Malchior came to the kingdom, claiming he too possessed great powers.

"The King is not the only one with magical powers!" The sorcerer claimed. "The universe is infinite and wise, so this has granted powers to a few chosen."

"If there is another one with marvelous powers. He might share his wisdom with me," the King said. "So let's him come here."

The King welcomed Malchior with open arms, hoping to learn more about his magical abilities.

But Malchior had ulterior motives. He wanted to overthrow the king and take control of the kingdom for himself. He saw the King as a threat to his power and needed to eliminate him.

There can't be two with magical powers here. One of us should rule, not two! Malchior thought.

One day, the sorcerer presented himself in the court. He invited the King to show his mettle and the strength of his magical powers by going through the darkness.

"What is the reward of going down to the depths of darkness?" The King asked.

"You will put under trial your power and wisdom to defeat evil. Once you defeat it, you will back with a pearl of great wisdom, and will show to your people your greatness," Malchior answered.

Malchior uttered this word. *"Consopite" "Consopite" Consopite."* And the sorcerer put a spell on the king, trapping him in a deep sleep.

The King descended in a spiral downwards to the depths, feeling trapped in a dark and lonely land. Despite this, he started walking, hoping to find a ray of light that would be a dimensional door. After wandering for a while, he still hadn't found any sign of light so he grew tired and sat down. But he knew that his strength lay in his bravery to be there. Suddenly, a ray of light appeared, and he walked towards it, entering into another dimension.

The kingdom was plunged into darkness, and Malchior declared himself the new ruler.

"As the King is not supposed to come back. I declare myself the new king."

Upon entering this dimension, he was presented with magnificent and gilded worlds, which he could rule by worshipping the demons that offered treasures to him.

The King's power lay in his adherence to his principles and his loyalty to his subordinates. "I will not compromise my beliefs and hand myself over to the forces of evil," declared the King. "Furthermore, my ego will not dictate the fate of my subordinates, nor mine."

However, the King's magic still lived within the kingdom. The animals could still hear his whispers in the wind, and the plants still thrived under his influence. The people of the kingdom called out to the king, desperate for his return.

Following those words, the King was escorted to a different location, where he heard a whisper, "You are going to spend eternity here."

"I accept my fate, but my resolve will assist me in discovering an escape route," the King replied. "The Universe will decide!"

After many long years in his slumber, the King finally woke up, restored to his full power. He did what he had to do to save his kingdom.

"I am back to rule my kingdom and my people again." Malchior, who had been trying to lead the King into darkness, realized that he had failed. The King had overcome all the obstacles and temptations with wisdom and strength. As a result, Malchior was stripped of his power and turned to dust.

The king who engaged in a magical battle with Malchior, ultimately defeated him.

After the rightful ruler regained control, the kingdom was thriving with magic once again. This story teaches us that magic resides within every one of us, and we can achieve anything if we use it wisely, without feeling the need to prove ourselves to others, but rather to ourselves.

ARTHUR

Arthur was a master magician who wowed crowds with his amazing displays of illusion every night. He had a charming personality, a quick wit, and an arsenal of magical tricks that seemed to be never-ending. He was so skilled and practiced that people often accused him of having actual supernatural powers.

There were rumors circulating that the magician possessed evil powers and had made a deal with evil for personal gain. Arthur argued that people often confuse the manifestation of their being with dark or gloomy powers.

Arthur had grown up as a shy and introverted kid, but he had discovered his love for magic at an early age and it had become his obsession. In his teenage years, he had worked as an assistant for a local magician, learning the tricks of the trade.

A desperate old woman once went to the local magician's studio seeking help. She explained that her daughter's son was ill and dying, and she hoped that the magician could restore her grandson's health. However, the magician replied that he was an illusionist, not a miracle worker. He couldn't change somebody's karma.

"I'm sorry to say this, but if this is what your daughter and her son have to go through, I can't prevent it," he said.

This was the paramount lesson that Arthur learned from the magician.

It wasn't long before he realized that he had a natural talent for it, and he began to develop his own signature style.

Arthur started performing at small events like birthday parties and local fairs before eventually making it to larger stages. As his career took off, he began receiving offers from prestigious venues all over the world. He became known for his jaw-dropping performances, his incredible showmanship, and his versatility as a magician.

Despite his success, Arthur remained humble and dedicated to improving his craft.

"Nobody is better than the other," Arthur always used to say. *"Besides, the miracle is oneself."*

He was always innovating and coming up with new ideas for his performances, which kept his audiences engaged and excited.

One day, while performing at a packed theater in Paris, Arthur's magic show took an unexpected and unusual turn. He disappeared on stage, and when he reappeared, he was holding a small crystal ball in his hand. He looked at it as if mesmerized and then placed it on a table in front of him.

Suddenly, images began to appear in the crystal ball, like scenes from another world. The audience was captivated, and Arthur took them on a journey through a mystical land, full of wonder and enchantment.

When the show was over, the crowd erupted into thunderous applause, and Arthur took his final bow. He knew that he had pushed the boundaries of what was possible as a magician, and he felt proud of what he had accomplished.

Arthur left the stage, feeling elated and fulfilled. He had always believed that magic was about more than just performing tricks; it was about creating an experience that would stay with your audience long after they left the theater. And with the reaction he had just received, he knew that he had achieved just that.

As he always said. *"You are the miracle!"*

ASTRID

Astrid had always been fascinated with astrology. As a child, she would often stare up at the stars in wonder, trying to decipher the secrets they held. As she grew up, she never lost her passion for astrology and pursued it as a career.

Her mother scolded her for wasting time staring at the sky. "I don't," Astrid replied. "I find secrets hidden in the stars."

In her early twenties, Astrid opened a small shop in the heart of the city, where she practiced astrology and sold unique astrological items. Her shop quickly became popular within the city, and many came to see her for consultations and advice.

She used to tell her customers, "Astrology is merely a means of guidance. The decision is still yours."

One day, a young woman named Emily came into the shop, looking for guidance. Emily was struggling in her personal and professional life, and she was searching for answers.

Astrid consulted the stars and analyzed Emily's birth chart, giving her valuable insights and offering practical advice.

Astrid advised that since the sun is in House 10, she should seize the opportunity to pursue the new professional opportunity that has come her way. "This position in the new company will help you achieve your goals and allow you to showcase yourself with strength and authority," said Astrid.

Emily was fascinated by the accuracy of Astrid's predictions and was eager to continue learning about astrology.

Over the next few weeks, Emily became a regular at Astrid's shop, soaking up as much knowledge as she could. As she delved deeper into the world of astrology, she started to notice changes in her life.

"He is a Scorpio, so he must be a great lover," Emily said. Astrid then asked, "Are you looking for a long-term partner or just a temporary fling?" The astrologist announced that Emily's relationship with the Pisces person in house 4 is well-aspected. However, she advised Emily to follow her heart and consider the value of every relationship offer that comes her way.

Her relationships improved, her work became more fulfilling, and she felt at peace with herself.

Eventually, Emily became so passionate about astrology that she decided to pursue it as a career. With Astrid's guidance, she became a skilled astrologer and opened her own shop, continuing Astrid's legacy.

Years passed, and Astrid's shop became a prominent institution in the city. She had become a mentor to many aspiring astrologers and had helped countless individuals find their paths in life.

Astrid knew that the stars held infinite secrets, and she dedicated her life to eking out the answers. She saw astrology as a window into the universe, and she felt happy knowing that she was able to help others navigate through its mysteries.

THE FORTUNE TELLER

Lena was a respected fortune teller in her small town. People would come to her for readings, and she was known for her accurate predictions. Everyone trusted her and looked up to her as a wise woman.

One day, a young couple came into Lena's shop, seeking her guidance. They were planning on getting married, and they wanted to know if it was the right decision.

Lena carefully studied the cards and predicted a long, prosperous marriage filled with love and happiness, warning them to be mindful of how they reflect on one another. "One is a mirror for another. So, watch out!"

The couple left the shop feeling reassured and confident about their future together.

However, months later, the couple returned to Lena's shop, unhappy and distressed. Their marriage was falling apart, and they were wondering how the prediction could have been so wrong. Lena was shocked and couldn't believe what she was hearing.

"Did you read well our cards," said the girl.

"I just predicted the events as these were shown then," the fortune teller said.

She had never made a mistake before, and she had always been known for her accurate readings. The fortune teller offered to do another reading for the couple but found that the outcome was still the same: their marriage was doomed to fail.

Feeling guilty and ashamed, Lena apologized to the couple and refunded their payment. She couldn't explain why the prediction had been wrong, but it was clear that her reading had been inaccurate.

This was a turning point for Lena. She began to doubt her abilities and question if she was truly meant to be a fortune teller. She took a break from her business and spent time reflecting on her life.

During this time, she realized that her mistake had been in assuming that the future was set in stone. She had failed to recognize that people have the power to choose their own paths in life and that a prediction is not a guarantee.

Lena came to the realization that the reason for the couple's failed marriage was due to the fact that living together frequently, making joint decisions, and negotiating interests require a shared set of values and a common vision for life. In the absence of these, it becomes challenging to come to an agreement, make compromises, or even understand each other's perspectives and choices.

The couple's relationship was doomed because they did not share a common direction.

Lena returned to her business with a newfound understanding and humility. She approached her readings differently, always emphasizing that the future is not fixed, and that people have the power to change it. Lena may have made a mistake, but it led her to a greater awareness and more compassionate approach towards her clients.

MIA

Mia had always felt a spiritual connection to the world around her. She would often spend hours in nature, soaking up the energy of the trees and the sky. She felt that there was something greater than herself out there, something that she couldn't quite put into words.

As she grew older, Mia's curiosity about spirituality deepened. She read books about different religions, attended meditation classes, and sought out spiritual teachers who could help her on her journey.

One day, Mia met a wise elder who told her about a mystical land far, far away. The elder spoke about how the land was teeming with spiritual energy, and that the people who lived there were deeply connected to the universe.

The wise elder shared that being in certain locations on Earth can have a profound impact on your energy and spirituality. "By altering the layers of your own energy, you will be able to deepen your spiritual journey. The Universe will open doors to wisdom and you will make progress on your spiritual path."

Mia was strongly drawn to visit this land and decided to embark on a journey to reach there. She traveled for several days across seas and mountains until she finally arrived at the land where spirituality thrived.

As soon as she set foot in the land, Mia felt a deep sense of calm. She was surrounded by beautiful gardens, towering trees, and crystal-clear streams. The welcoming people of the land embraced her with open arms and invited her to participate in their spiritual practices.

Mia spent many weeks in the land of spirituality, learning new practices, and discovering new ways to connect with the universe. She felt a sense of belonging that she had never felt before, and she knew that this is where she was meant to be.

Eventually, Mia needed to return home, but she knew that she would carry the teachings and practices of the spiritual land with her always.

As we gain a deeper understanding of our position in the universe, we start to reap the rewards of a profound link between spirituality and nature. This connection can bring about a higher level of gratitude towards things as they are, and a greater awareness and comprehension of sustainable practices, she learned.

She returned to her old life, but everything had changed. She saw the world through new eyes, and she was able to approach every situation with more understanding and compassion than before.

Mia had always felt a spiritual connection, but it wasn't until she found the land of spirituality that she truly discovered the depths of her own being. She had discovered a new way of life, and she knew that it was something that she would never let go of.

DR. HUGHES

Once upon a time, in a small town nestled between rolling hills, there was a palmologist named Dr. Hughes. Although her profession was scientific, she had a unique talent for analyzing the lines and ridges of people's hands to determine their personality traits, health conditions, and future fortunes. This special ability was in contrast with her rational mind and professional work.

Dr. Hughes had a cozy little office with dim lighting, comfortable chairs, and shelves filled with books about palm reading. She would greet each of her clients with a warm smile and invite them to sit down, holding their hands gently but firmly in hers.

One day, a young woman named Emily walked into Dr. Hughes' office. Emily had been feeling lost and unsure of her path in life, and she hoped that Dr. Hughes could offer some insight. As Dr. Hughes began to study Emily's hands, she saw that they had a unique combination of creativity and determination.

"Your strength lies in your determination and persistence!" Dr. Hughes announced.

With a twinkle in her eye, Dr. Hughes told Emily that she had the potential to be a great artist and that her artistic skills could take her far in life.

Emily admitted to never exploring any artistic style. Dr. Hughes recommended considering her interests in developing skills.

Anyway, Emily was surprised but thrilled by Dr. Hughes' assessment, and she decided to take her words to heart.

Over the next few years, Emily worked hard to hone her artistic skills and began to see success in her career. She was grateful to Dr. Hughes for opening her eyes to her potential and setting her on this path.

Dr. Hughes continued to help many more people over the years, offering them guidance and insight through her palm readings, though. This craft didn't have to do anything with any scientific or rational thought. However, she knew that while the lines in people's hands could suggest certain traits and tendencies, ultimately it was up to each individual to shape their own destiny. And by helping them see their potential, Dr. Hughes felt that she was doing her small part to create a better world.

Dr. Hughes was known far and wide for her expertise in analyzing the lines and ridges of people's hands to determine their personality traits, health conditions, and future fortunes.

MADAME VERA

Once upon a time, in a bustling city, there was a tarot card reader named Madam Vera. She was known far and wide for her psychic abilities and uncanny accuracy in reading the mystical cards.

Madam Vera had a small room in the heart of the city, where she would invite her clients to sit down and shuffle the deck of tarot cards. As the cards were shuffled, Madam Vera would hold her hands over them, feeling their energy and listening to their whispers.

Then, with a flourish, she would lay out the cards in a particular pattern and begin to interpret their meaning. She would take her clients on a journey through the imagery on the cards, explaining how each card represented their past, present, and future.

Madam Vera possessed extraordinary psychic abilities and was almost always accurate in her predictions. However, her purpose in life was shaken when a stubborn woman came to her, challenging her mystic power. Despite Madam Vera being right about the woman's past and present, the woman questioned why Madam Vera was still enclosed in a room, instead of using her gift for her own benefit. Madam Vera was left speechless and unable to refute the woman's argument.

Anyway, one day, a man named David came to see Madam Vera. He was in a state of distress, feeling lost and confused about what direction to take in life. As Madam Vera turned over the cards, she saw that David was going through a major life transition and that a new beginning was just around the corner.

She explained that while change could be scary, it was also an opportunity to grow and expand one's horizons.

"Changes always scare us," Madame Vera said. "However, as you navigate through tough times, your character will be shaped and you will unravel the mysteries of the Universe about attraction and manifestation. In other words, you will learn how to become a miracle worker."

She saw that David had a creative spark within him that was waiting to be unleashed and encouraged him to pursue his passions.

With a renewed sense of hope, David left Madam Vera's room feeling lighter and energized. He went on to take her advice and soon found his calling as a writer, discovering a talent he never knew he had.

David's writings became a source of motivation for those in need.

The tarot reader's purpose is to guide and assist others in finding their path in life, rather than seeking personal gain.

Madam Vera continued to help many more people over the years, using her tarot cards as a tool for self-discovery and empowerment. She knew that while the cards may seem mysterious and mystical on the surface, at their core they were simply a reflection of the human experience – a reminder that we all have the power to create our own destiny.

A CLAIRVOYANT

In a quiet village nestled among the hills, there lived a clairvoyant named Cassandra. She had an exceptional gift of seeing and sensing things that others couldn't.

Cassandra's gift didn't come without its downsides. Often, people in the town would look at her with disdain and as an outsider. It was rumored that she had obtained her extraordinary powers through the use of evil forces. Some believed that these powers were of a diabolical nature. Those who sought her assistance were said to worship evil in order to have their wishes granted. However, Cassandra knew her place in life, and she was content with the fact that she can see things that others cannot.

The mayor was distressed about the state of the town. The crops were dying, and people didn't sleep well at night. He had tried everything he could, but nothing seemed to work. In fact, many believed it was a punishment from God for Cassandra's gloomy acts and worship of evil. So, out of desperation, he decided to turn to Cassandra, the only person who could possibly tell him what was happening.

Cassandra agreed to help and sat down with the mayor. "What brings you here?" She asked. However, in no time, she had a vision. She saw that the town's water source had been infected by chemicals from a nearby factory.

This is what Cassandra said to the mayor. "The factory is the source of the problem. It disposes of all the harmful chemicals in the water, making it contaminated. The contamination is not a result of God's punishment, as many people in town believe."

The mayor responded by saying. "Thank you for bringing this to my attention. I will investigate the matter."

Cassandra was satisfied not only because she was able to help, but also because she was able to clear up any misunderstandings about her abilities."

To the mayor's surprise, Cassandra's clairvoyance was right. The factory had been knowingly discharging dangerous chemicals into the water source, leading to the town's current plight. The mayor immediately called a town meeting to address the issue, and they marched to the factory to confront its owner.

With the factory shut down and the water source cleaned up, the town began to prosper again. As word spread, Cassandra began to earn the respect of the townspeople. They started to believe that her gift was divine and that she was meant to use her extraordinary powers to help others and show gratitude to the Creator.

She no longer felt like an outsider but had become an essential part of the town's wellbeing.

News of Cassandra's gift traveled far and wide. People from other towns and cities started coming to seek her help in solving various mysteries and problems plaguing their places. Cassandra embraced her gift and became a beacon of hope for many people in need, always ready to help in any way she knew how through her clairvoyance.

KAIDA

Once upon a time, there was a tiny village in a dense forest. The villagers believed that the forest was filled with spirits who could both haunt and protect them. They left offerings for the spirits at the edge of the forest and avoided going deep into the woods.

One day, a brave young girl named Kaida decided to explore the forest. She wanted to find out whether the spirits were real or just a myth. She walked for hours, admiring the beauty of the trees and listening to the birds singing. As the sun began to set, she stumbled upon a clearing, and there, she saw them – the spirits.

The spirits were beautiful and gentle creatures that floated in the air. They welcomed Kaida with open arms and showed her around their magical world. There were hundreds of them, each with a unique personality and skill. Some could control the elements of nature, others could conjure up spells, and some could even travel through time. Kaida was shown several breathtaking and enchanted kingdoms by others.

Kaida was fascinated by everything she saw. She learned that the spirits were not evil, but rather they protected the forest and the village. They were playful and mischievous, but they had a deep love for all living things.

As the night grew darker, Kaida realized that it was time for her to head back to the village. The spirits wished her farewell and sent her on her way with a gift. They gave her a magical stone that would protect her from evil and bring her good luck. Besides, the stone proved to be helpful to the villagers. Whenever Kaida held it, she could provide solutions to the problems of the villagers.

Kaida returned to the village with her newfound knowledge and treasure. She shared her experience with the villagers, who were both amazed and grateful. They left more offerings for the spirits at the edge of the forest and started to understand the importance of respecting and honoring them.

From then on, the village and the spirits lived in harmony. The spirits continued to protect the village, and the villagers respected and admired them. Kaida had not only uncovered the truth about the spirits but had also taught her people a valuable lesson about trust and acceptance.

THE SAINTS

In a small town in Cuba, a young girl named

Elena grew up hearing stories about Santeria from

her grandmother. She was fascinated by the idea

of communicating with the gods and saw the

rituals as almost magical.

One day, while wandering in the forest, Elena

stumbled upon a group of people at a ceremony.

Some were chanting prayers and songs to call

upon orichas and spirits, while others were

performing esoteric rituals. These were

connecting with the gods in the same way she had

heard about. She was intrigued and approached

them with curiosity.

"What are you doing?" Elena asked.

They welcomed her with open arms and explained that they were a group of Santeria practitioners.

Elena was quickly absorbed in their group, where she discovered everything she had been missing. They taught her how to connect with the Orishas, the gods of the Santeria religion, and how to honor them.

During one of their rituals, they performed an herbal bath followed by creating a circle where the person stands. Then, the signature of the saint we made with a product called bemba in Palo and cascarilla in Santería. The person was then sprinkled with certain products and drops of the sacrificed animal's blood that were placed on their head and feet. The ritual included other things that were done to the saints and the saint was asked for their food sacrifice. For instance, the participant said: "Papa Elegguá, here is your daughter, who comes to offer you a little food to help you, she needs your help. Are you going to help her? Do you accept her little food?" After the sacrifice, the participant asked the saint if they were satisfied with what they were given and if they needed anything else. The saint required liquor, and the participant provided it. Finally, the participant asked the saint if they needed anything else and if he could retire with their blessing.

Every week, they gathered in their sacred space, danced to the beat of the drums, and chanted beautiful songs in honor of the Orishas.

Months into it, Elena was initiated into the religion and dedicated her life to it. She studied with the group of Santeria practitioners and learned everything, from making offerings to performing the rituals. She found peace in Santeria, and it became her life's purpose.

As her knowledge of the religion grew, her family began to notice a positive change in her spirit. Elena's grandmother, who had introduced her to Santeria, became proud of her and watched her grow into a beautiful and respected Santeria priestess.

Elena always followed her grandmother's advice to respect the will of saints and spirits. She added that guidance from above was available, but the decision was still Elena's.

Years went by, and Elena continued to be devoted to the religion of Santeria. She built a new extended family around her, a group of fellow practitioners who shared the same values of respect, love, and devotion to the Orishas.

Eventually, when Elena's time on earth came to an end, she had traveled the world sharing her experiences, teaching the religion of Santeria and carrying her group's teachings. Her memory lived on, as those she taught continued to practice her traditions for generations to come.

Elena's spirit lived on in those she taught – they believed that her love and devotion to the Orishas were a most powerful force and maintained the same faith in her memory.

65